Lights Out at Camp What-a-Nut

Lights Out at Camp What-a-Nut

Paul McCusker

PUBLISHING
Colorado Springs, Colorado

LIGHTS OUT AT CAMP WHAT-A-NUT

Copyright © 1993 by Focus on the Family

Library of Congress Cataloging-in-Publication Data applied for.

Published by Focus on the Family Publishing, Colorado Springs, CO 80920.

Distributed in the U.S.A. and Canada by Word Books, Dallas, Texas.

Editors: Deena Davis and Larry K. Weeden
Interior illustrations: Jeff Stoddard
Interior design: Tim Howard
Cover illustration: Jeff Haynie

Printed in the United States of America

93 94 95 96 97/10 9 8 7 6 5 4 3 2 1

To John G. –
in memory of those wonderful
days and nights at Camp W

Fans of the audio and video series of **Adventures in Odyssey** *may wonder why some of their favorite characters aren't found in these novels. The answer is simple: the novels take place in a period of time prior to the audio or video series.*

Contents

CHAPTER ONE

Home Again

The banner "Welcome to Odyssey Municipal Airport!" stretched across the airline gate, ready to greet the passengers on the approaching plane. Mark Prescott leaned across his mother's seat to get a clear look out the window. Although the pane was dotted with raindrops from yet another late August storm, he could see the banner and felt his heart leap at the name "Odyssey."

"Are you glad to be back?" Julie, his mother, asked.

Mark nodded.

Julie rubbed Mark's back. "I was just thinking how nice it is to be home again. Funny, huh?—thinking about Odyssey as home."

Mark understood what she meant. When his parents separated the previous June, Mark was sure nothing worse

1

could ever happen to him. That is, until Julie moved Mark to her grandmother's house in Odyssey, halfway across the country from his father, Richard, and their home in Washington, D.C. Then Mark *knew* it was the end of the world.

But that was last June.

In the three months since then, he had made new friends, enjoyed Odyssey's gentle charm, and taken part in some exciting adventures (including taking a trip in a time machine and solving a mystery). Slowly, Mark felt less like a stranger and more like a welcome friend. By August, it was as if he'd always been there—and always would be.

Mark and Julie followed the crowd of passengers from the plane to the baggage-claim area. A horn sounded a warning blast, and the conveyor belt loudly whirred to life. Mark stood nearby, grabbing their luggage when it came past. They tossed the cases onto a cart and pushed it to the long-term parking area where Julie had parked the car only a few days before.

Only a few days? It seems longer than that, Mark thought, then said so out loud.

"Did it seem long because you didn't enjoy yourself?" Julie asked as she closed the trunk.

"I guess so," Mark said with a shrug. "It wasn't as much fun as I thought it would be. It's like . . . our house wasn't ours anymore."

Julie nodded her head, a lock of her long, brown hair falling across her face. "I understand. Everything looked the

same as it did before we left, but it seemed different somehow. Once or twice, I felt like I was a visitor in a museum."
She started the car and backed out of the parking space.

"All my old friends were either away on vacation or they didn't want to see me," Mark complained. That bothered him a lot. Somehow it didn't seem fair that they went on with their lives without him being there to give his approval.

Julie paid the parking attendant, wound up her window, and pulled away. "That's the hardest part. When you go away, you think everyone should suddenly stop in their tracks and never do anything important without you. You think you're the only one who can change or make new friends or have new experiences. And when you come back, it's a shock to find out that their lives kept going—just like yours did."

"Yeah, but Mike Adams is hanging around Tom Nelson! They couldn't stand each other before!"

Julie laughed and said, "Just like you never thought you could have a girl as a friend."

His mom was referring to Patti Eldridge, a girl who had become Mark's closest friend in Odyssey during the summer.

"That's different," Mark replied. He stared out the passenger window thoughtfully. "And I thought you and Dad . . ." He glanced down at his lap uncomfortably.

Julie finished his sentence: "You thought your dad and I would get back together again. I know."

She was right. The reason they had gone to Washington,

D.C., in the first place was so that Mark's mom and dad could iron out their differences. But by the time Richard dropped Mark and Julie off at the airport for their return trip to Odyssey, it was clear that wasn't going to happen.

"I'm sorry, Mark," Julie said. "I really thought your dad and I would work it all out. I thought this trip would be the end of our separation. I know you're disappointed."

"Wars have ended quicker than you two getting back together," Mark said as they drove away from the airport.

Julie smiled wearily in return. "You have to be patient. You may not see the improvements, but they're there."

"Then why aren't we together again?"

"Because we're not ready," she answered. "I won't get back with your father until I'm sure we're ready."

"But that's what you and Dad keep saying!"

"I know. But some things came up in our counseling session that we have to figure out." Julie sighed. "You wouldn't understand."

"What wouldn't I understand?" Mark snapped. "Why do you always think I don't understand?"

Julie glanced at Mark, a pained expression on her face.

"I'm sorry," Mark said. "I didn't mean to be so sharp."

Julie acknowledged the apology with a nod, then reached across the seat to touch Mark's hand. "It's all leading somewhere, Mark. You have to trust us. We've needed this time to mend our wounds."

Mark shot her an ornery look, then said, "Maybe you should buy some Band-Aids."

She pinched him playfully and drove on.

CHAPTER TWO

Another Trip

At home, Mark hurriedly unpacked his case. He was eager to talk to Patti, to tell her everything that had happened. He smiled at the thought of Patti listening attentively to the disappointment and frustration he felt. He imagined her reaction. She would be sympathetic. She would understand how he felt. *In other words, she'll do all the things a friend is supposed to do,* Mark thought. She wasn't at all like those uncaring friends he left back in Washington.

But Patti wasn't home. Her mother reminded Mark that she had left to go to Camp What-a-Nut, a summer camp in the mountains. She'd be gone a week.

"Oh no," Mark whispered. He had forgotten all about it. What was he going to do for a whole week?

7

The situation got worse when Mark walked downtown to Whit's End. It was an ice cream parlor and discovery emporium for kids, filled with room after room of displays, inventions, play areas, a library, and workshops. It also boasted having the "largest train set in the county." Mark, like most of the kids in Odyssey, loved going there—not only for the fun, but also because of John Avery Whittaker, the owner. Whit (as he was best known) was a kind, generous, and wise man who used Whit's End as a way to help kids. Sometimes it was enough for kids to simply have a place to play, but Whit often listened to the kids' problems and offered a word of advice. He'd helped Mark on several occasions.

But Whit wasn't there when Mark arrived. He had gone to camp, too. Tom Riley, Whit's best friend, stood behind the ice cream counter and cheerfully served customers. "Howya doin'?" Tom asked Mark in his gentle drawl.

Mark shrugged and answered, "Okay, I guess. Patti and Whit are gone."

Tom tugged at a loose strap on his overalls and buttoned it up again. "Left for camp while you were in Washington, huh?"

"Yeah," Mark replied, cradling his head in his hands sadly. "I forgot all about it."

"Plenty of other people are still around," Tom observed.

"But not Patti or Whit," Mark complained.

Tom watched Mark thoughtfully for a moment, then snapped his fingers as if he had just thought of a great idea. "Why don't *you* go to camp?" he asked.

Mark lifted his head. "It's too late . . . isn't it?"

"I don't think it's ever too late to go to Camp What-a-Nut. Most years they have plenty of room." Tom leaned close to Mark. "I'm sure Whit would be glad to see you. In fact, he was saying just the other day how different the place seems when you're not around."

Mark's spirits brightened. "He said that about *me?*"

Mark found it hard to believe considering the tension between them right before Mark left for Washington. Mark had stayed at Whit's house for a couple of days after Julie left. While he was there, he disobeyed Whit by sneaking into a locked room, where he broke a treasured heirloom of Whit's. Mark apologized and Whit forgave him, but it didn't take away from the surprise of Tom's words.

"Yep, that's what he said." Tom nodded and hooked his thumbs in his overall straps. One of them came loose.

****

"Camp *what?*" Julie asked as she leaned across the kitchen table.

"Not Camp *What* — Camp *What-a-Nut*," Mark corrected her.

"That's a silly name," she said.

Mark couldn't argue. He didn't know where the camp got its name and wasn't sure it was important at the moment. "I was thinking that maybe it would be fun to go . . . you know, before school starts."

He nearly choked on the word *school*—and even felt a tightening in his chest at the realization that summer was ending so quickly.

"But I don't know anything about it," Julie said, spreading her arms. "Where is it? How much does it cost to go?"

Mark pushed a brochure that Tom Riley had given him across the table. Julie looked surprised, then picked it up.

"Camp What-a-Nut, nestled next to the beautiful Lake Manitou in the Green Ridge Mountains, offers sound moral teaching combined with recreational facilities and large dormitories for the campers. Archery, canoeing, swimming, softball, horseback riding, and a number of crafts are all just a part of the fun found at Camp What-a-Nut . . ." Her voice trailed off as she continued to read to herself.

Mark shook his leg impatiently.

"Hm," she finally said.

Mark looked up expectantly.

"Well . . . " she began as she set the brochure on the table again.

Mark stopped pumping his leg.

"If you really want to go, I guess you can."

Mark shouted and hugged her.

CHAPTER THREE

Camp
What-a-Nut

From the porch of Pine Lodge, Camp What-a-Nut's main cabin, Mark watched his mother carefully maneuver her car past the potholes in the dirt road that led away from camp. He waved, but he knew she wouldn't wave back. She wouldn't dare take her hands off the steering wheel for fear of landing in one of the holes.

He leaned forward and rested his arms on the large, brown log that served as the porch's handrail. From this vantage point, Mark could see most of the camp. Several small cabins, built with the same kind of logs, circled the driveway at the center of the camp like a wagon train under

Indian attack. Beyond the circle, a carpet of thick grass stretched toward playing fields, a fenced-in swimming pool, and a large stable. The green carpet suddenly gave way to a wall of trees that covered the mountain like badly combed hair.

To the left, a large, blue lake twinkled in the sun as if someone had thrown glitter all over it. He longed for a closer look. The air was fresh with the scent of pine. Mark hummed softly with the serenity of it all.

Then a screen door slammed behind him.

"Okay, Matt," Mr. Gunnoe, an assistant director of the camp, said.

"Mark," Mark corrected him.

Mr. Gunnoe adjusted his glasses and looked closer at the registration slip in his hand. "Mark. Right. We went over the rules of the camp while your mother was here, we took care of the medical release, we got your tuition paid up in full, your suitcase is right here, and—let's see—we'll put you in Wabana."

"Wabana?"

"That's the name of the cabin you'll stay in. Follow me."

"Where is everybody?" Mark asked as they walked across the circle and under the flag pole that marked its center. An American flag flapped in the soft breeze with a sound like birds' wings.

"They're at lunch in the cafeteria—over there." Mr. Gunnoe pointed to a long building just off the circle of cabins.

Unlike everything else, the building was made of large sheets of metal bolted together. It reminded Mark of an Army boot camp he once saw on television. A large bell in a wooden frame sat in front of the building.

"They ring the bell when it's time to eat," Mr. Gunnoe added. He held open the screen door of Wabana as Mark lugged his suitcase into the dark, cool room. The cabin was filled with bunk beds, lined exactly opposite each other along two walls. Each bed was made, except for one at the very end. On that one, the covers were tossed aside, and clothes were strewn about. It was a startling contrast to the rest of the neatness.

"Disgusting, isn't it?" Mr. Gunnoe said, obviously noticing Mark's gaze. "That's Joe's bed."

Mark frowned and asked, "Joe Devlin?"

"You know him? Too bad for you. Your bed is right next to his."

Mark groaned loudly.

"Sorry, but it's the only one left in this cabin, which is the only one designated for your age group." Mr. Gunnoe pulled a pencil from behind his ear and scribbled on a piece of paper.

Mark dropped his suitcase and glanced again at the disheveled bed nearby. He was genuinely surprised that someone like Joe Devlin would come to camp. More than that, he dreaded the idea of being so close to Joe. They had had several arguments since Mark arrived in Odyssey; one even led to a fight. It wasn't Mark's fault, though. Joe Devlin was a bully.

"The kid's a terror," Mr. Gunnoe said. "We've already reprimanded him once. Twice more and he'll be expelled from camp."

"Good," Mark whispered.

Mr. Gunnoe showed Mark where the toilets and showers were, then gave him a sheet of paper with the afternoon's schedule. It gave Mark the option of taking a swimming, archery, or woodworking class. Mark decided he'd try the archery.

Just like Robin Hood, he thought.

****

Until Mark saw Patti walk toward him from the cafeteria, he had forgotten that their last conversation ended with her slamming the phone down in his ear. It happened right before Mark went to see his father. He had been staying at Whit's house, and Patti had called him at the wrong time (just as he was about to solve the mystery of Whit's locked attic door). He was rude to her, and she got mad and hung up.

Now he wondered what Patti would say to him—*if* she spoke to him at all. He stood perfectly still and waited for her to get closer. A tight smile stretched across his lips and froze in place. "Hi, Patti," he squeaked when she was within earshot.

She was dressed in her favorite outfit: faded jeans, t-shirt, and baseball cap. Her right arm was in a cast because of an accident a few weeks before. It was covered with good wishes and signatures. Mark braced himself as she stopped directly in front of him. She tipped the baseball cap away from her forehead. Her eyes burned into his.

"How's it going?" Mark asked.

Patti slugged him in the arm.

"Hey!" he cried out.

"That's for being so mean to me on the phone!" she shouted. "Now apologize!"

"That *hurt!*" Mark whined.

Patti punched him in the other arm. "Apologize!" she demanded.

"All right, all right, I'm sorry," Mark said. He glanced around quickly to make sure no one had seen them.

"Say you're *really* sorry," she insisted, raising her fist.

"I'm *really* sorry," Mark said, then nearly whispered, "*Really, really* sorry, Patti. I mean it."

Mark was sincere, and Patti knew him well enough to realize it. Her tone softened. "Okay. So, what happened to you?"

Mark wasn't sure if she meant at Whit's house or in Washington. Either way, he didn't think it was the right time to explain. "All kinds of things. I'll tell you later. Do you like camp?"

"Uh huh," she replied. "Did you come up to visit for the day?"

Mark shook his head. "I'm here for the rest of the week."

Mark expected her to be pleased with the news. Instead, she frowned and said, "Oh, really?"

"Yeah. What's wrong with that?"

"Nothing," she said in a voice that meant *something*. She screwed her face up as if she was thinking hard about whether to tell Mark what was on her mind.

Perhaps she would have if they hadn't been interrupted by a tall, red-headed boy who ran in their direction and called Patti's name. He had a lean, athletic build that was well-displayed beneath his muscle shirt and gym shorts. Though Mark guessed he was only a couple of years older than either him or Patti, his voice had already changed to a deeper, more teenage pitch.

"I've been looking for you," he puffed as he wiped the sweat from his brow.

"Hi, David." Patti giggled strangely. "I was just talking to—" Patti stopped, then looked at Mark with wide, surprised eyes. She had clearly forgotten his name.

"I'm Mark," Mark said.

Patti blushed. "Yeah. Mark. And this is David Boyer. He works here. At the camp, I mean. He sets up tables for the meals and teaches some of the classes and . . . oh, he does everything."

"Hi," Mark said uneasily. Patti was acting very weird all of a sudden. If Mark didn't know better, he'd swear she was gushing.

"Is this the kid you told me about?" David asked Patti.

Patti cleared her throat and answered, "Well, uh—"

"You shouldn't have acted like that on the phone," David said to Mark. "It wasn't very polite."

Mark thought of the two punches Patti had given him in the arm and wondered if David would consider *them* polite. "I know," he said.

David turned his attention to Patti again. "We're gonna be late for the afternoon classes."

"You're right," Patti answered with a lilt in her voice.

Mark watched as David and Patti walked away. David apparently said something amusing, because Patti threw her head back and laughed. Her baseball cap fell off, and she bent down to retrieve it. Before she could, however, David deftly snapped it up. He handed it to her in a gentlemanly manner. She shot an uncomfortable glance back at Mark, then went on her way.

I've never seen her act like that, Mark thought. Then it suddenly came back to him. He had. It wasn't long after they first met. She had asked him if he'd ever kissed a girl. And she had carved a heart with their initials into a tree.

"Oh no," Mark said out loud. He hoped she wasn't going through another one of those weird girl things the way she did then. It nearly wrecked their friendship. *And who is that David guy, anyway, to tell me how to be polite?* Mark shoved his hands into his jeans pockets and ambled to archery class.

David was his teacher.

CHAPTER FOUR

The Old Dock

Mark didn't feel much like Robin Hood as he fumbled with the bow, thumped the bow-string as it caught in his fingers, and dropped arrows like a clumsy oaf. He never got near the target.

David was patient. Even helpful. But it was too late. Mark was already determined not to like him, though he couldn't have said why. Patti also took the archery class, but she couldn't do much because of her cast.

"Patti and I like Robin Hood," Mark announced. "We sometimes play it at home."

"Mark!" Patti cried out, red-faced.

"What?" Mark asked.

She sent a disapproving expression his way and shook her head. David didn't seem to notice.

After the class ended, Mark left quickly. He couldn't bear the way Patti gushed all over David. *She'll probably forget my name again,* he decided.

He frowned as he walked. What was Patti's problem? Why was she acting so strange? *I came all the way to camp to talk to her, and she has a . . .* Mark stopped. He was hung up on the word that would complete the sentence. He didn't want to believe it was true.

Patti has a boyfriend?

Mark shook his head. The idea was too new for him to fully appreciate what it meant. And in the back of his mind, he wondered, *Why does she need a boyfriend when she has me?*

It scared him. He pictured Patti spending all her time with David and never having any time for him. *Just like my old friends in Washington.*

Mark determined to put Patti and David out of his mind as he walked beyond the playing fields, past the young horseriders being led back to the stable by a leather-faced man in a cowboy hat. He went directly to the thing he'd wanted to see since arriving—Lake Manitou.

Under the bright sun, the gentle water swirled like icing on a lemon cake and lapped the ground near Mark's feet. Across the lake, Mark noticed scattered cabins—probably owned by rich tourists. A handful of small boats with sails thrust out like pigeons' chests rode the rise and fall of the current. A large bird appeared, floated above the water, then flew off again. He watched it move gracefully to his left, where it landed on a collection of twisted wood that stuck up from the water and reached out from shore for several yards. *A dock,* Mark guessed. But the wood was old and rotted and probably unable to bear more than a bird's weight.

His curiosity aroused, Mark walked the distance to the edge where the shore met the dock. A large sign warned him to go no farther because the dock was condemned, forbidden. "Stay away!" it shouted. The bird squawked and flew off. The dock seemed terribly lonely.

Lonely, maybe, but Mark wasn't alone. He heard talking—whispering—nearby. He followed the sound around a large pile of discarded lumber and stopped just short of being seen by the gathering of boys there.

"We're not supposed to go near it," one of the boys complained.

"That makes it even better," another boy replied. Mark recognized the voice. It was Joe Devlin. Mark strained to listen more closely.

Joe continued, "An initiation's no good if it's easy."

"I—I don't know," another boy said so softly that Mark could barely make out his words.

"You wanna be in my gang or not?" Joe asked.

No one answered.

"Look, kid," Joe said, "all you have to do is walk to the

end of that thing, turn around, and come back. Think you can handle it?"

Mark looked at the dock and tried to imagine the chances of success. It was falling apart, slanted, and slippery from the water that splashed between the wood pilings.

"No sweat," someone said.

Joe laughed. "You think you're so tough, but we'll see. Come on."

Realizing they were going to spot him, Mark jumped back and tried to pretend he was only just arriving. Joe was the first to emerge from behind the woodpile. He was surprised to see Mark and instantly sneered. "Hey! It's Mark Pressnot!"

The group of boys looked at him curiously.

Mark put his hands on his hips and asked, "What're you doing here, Joe?"

"That's for me to know and you to find out," Joe said, poking a finger into Mark's chest. "Unless you're spying on me. You're not spying on me, are you? Or maybe you're playing snitch for your buddy-buddy Mr. Whit's End?"

Mark didn't bother to answer, nor did Joe wait for one. He simply shoved Mark aside and walked on. One by one, his followers did the same. They looked like frightened puppies. *Just the kind of kids Joe Devlin likes to pick on*, Mark thought as he felt anew a deep loathing for Joe. He tried to guess which kid was crazy enough to agree to walk on the dock.

Mark turned back to the wreckage of the old dock. It couldn't be that hard to walk to the end and back, could it?

A bird let out a piercing scream overhead. Mark's skin crawled.

Yes. It could.

****

"Joe's been a real pain in the neck since camp started," Patti said as she stretched her legs and leaned back against a tree. "He's even worse than usual—if that's possible."

"Why?" Mark asked. He sat Indian-style as he plucked a fistful of grass and tossed it to one side absentmindedly.

Patti shrugged. "Who knows?"

"But how does he do it?" Mark asked.

"Do what?"

"Get a gang together so fast. He's only been here for two days, and already he has a whole group of kids around him." Mark was genuinely perplexed.

"I guess they attract each other. Kids looking for trouble will find other kids looking for trouble, and so they find trouble together."

Mark looked at her quizzically. He wasn't entirely sure that what she said made sense. But Patti didn't seem to notice. She was too busy examining the signatures on her cast. For a moment he felt a tinge of relief. He was glad he had caught up with her when David wasn't around. She seemed like her old self.

"It's like how I met David," she began.

His feeling of relief quickly disappeared. "Huh?"

She smiled. "I was looking for a tennis ball that I knocked over the fence, and—guess what he did."

"He handed it to you," Mark said dryly, then resumed plucking the grass.

"He handed it to me!" Patti giggled.

She was gushing again. *Maybe coming to camp wasn't such a good idea after all*, he thought. He yanked at another clump of grass and pulled it up, roots and all.

"Mark, have you ever been in love?"

"What!" Mark shrieked. "Snap out of it, Patti! Stop being so weird!"

Patti sat up. "I'm not being weird! There's nothing weird about being in love!"

"In love! With David? But you just met the guy!"

"That's what's so bizarre," Patti said significantly. "It's like we've *always* known each other. Like . . . we were *meant* for each other."

Mark groaned and fell backward onto the grass. "I don't believe it. You sound just like one of those gross black-and-white movies my mom likes to watch on TV. It's disgusting."

"You're just jealous," Patti said.

"I am not."

"I saw how you acted at archery class," she argued. "You acted like you were mad."

"That's only because I was getting sick to my stomach

watching you and David make goo-goo eyes at each other."

"You're jealous."

"I am not."

Patti reached over, touched Mark's arm, and spoke with a voice full of honey. "Mark, you don't have to be jealous. If David and I get married, you can come visit anytime you want. We'll still be friends."

"Married!" Mark cried out.

Just then the dinner bell clanged.

CHAPTER FIVE

Trouble with Joe

ark carried his tray along the food line and watched with wide eyes as the staff hastily threw scoops of something on the plates and handed them over the counter to each passing camper. It was an assembly line. Only Mark wasn't sure what they were assembling. The food was formless and void.

Patti asked Mark to sit with her and David, but he declined. Her voice was still full of that sickly sweet tone. He didn't want to lose his appetite.

He looked around for Whit but didn't see him. Mark thought it was unusual that he had been at the camp all day without seeing or hearing anything about him.

Mr. Gunnoe blew into a microphone mounted on a makeshift public address system. It made him sound as if he had a mouth full of cotton, and it whistled with feedback when he tried to speak louder. "Testing one . . . two . . . three . . . uh . . ." he said. After jiggling control knobs and re-adjusting the microphone, he announced that he would say grace for the food and then inform them about the long-awaited camp treasure hunt. A few of the campers cheered.

"Lord," he prayed, "for these and this which thine hand hath provided, we thank You and ask You to mumphilgree-berhoffasnagglenasson . . . "

His voice disappeared into a muffled ball of static. The public address system screeched high and loud and then fizzled into silence. Mr. Gunnoe cupped his hands around his mouth and shouted, "Bless this food! Amen!"

Mark found an empty stool at the end of a long, white table. It was the kind of table they could fold up after the meal and stand in a corner.

He didn't realize as he began to eat that he was so close to the very people he wanted to avoid. Two tables away, Patti gazed at David and giggled at nearly everything he said. Farther down Mark's own table, Joe was holding court with his gang. He spoke in a soft, threatening growl while they leaned over their plates, eyes fixed nervously on his every gesture.

Mark looked away and tried to figure his chances of sneaking off without Joe making a scene. It was too late.

"It's Pressnot again!" Joe said derisively. "This is the second time he's been hanging around us. Think he wants to join the gang?"

Tense laughter rippled around Joe's gang.

Mark grimaced and probed his food with a fork.

Joe stood up and came nearer. "I don't think he's tough enough. He hangs around a *girl* all the time."

"Get lost, Joe," Mark said.

Joe squeezed between two campers sitting across from Mark. They watched him anxiously as he leaned forward. "Oh, that's right. You don't hang around a girl anymore because she has a *new* boyfriend."

It was obvious he was talking about Patti and David. Mark clenched his teeth and told himself over and over that he shouldn't slug Joe in the mouth.

"How about it, Mark?" Joe hissed. "Do you think he's a good replacement for you? Does Patti think he *kisses* better than you?"

Mark pushed his fork into the stiff waves of mashed potatoes.

Joe spread his arms and announced to his gang, "Do you see, boys? I try to have a friendly conversation, and he ignores me." He suddenly pounded the table, causing the plates and cutlery to rattle, then walked back to his seat.

That was easy, Mark thought. *Why didn't I try ignoring him a long time ago?*

He glanced over at Patti and David again. They seemed

oblivious to the scene between Mark and Joe. Patti spoke quietly to David, then reached across the table and placed her hand on his forearm. Mark felt the scratch of a match against the lining of his stomach. It flickered into a flame that made his face turn red.

Splat. Something wet hit Mark on the cheek. He swiped at it and saw it was a kernel of corn. He looked over at Joe, who had a straw positioned against his smirking lips. It was aimed directly at Mark. Joe's gang laughed.

Mark felt the flame turn into a bonfire and skillfully tossed a scoop of mashed potatoes at Joe. It smacked him in the forehead. The smirk disappeared, and Joe grabbed his entire plate and hurled the contents at Mark. Mark retaliated with a half bowl of withered salad.

An all-out war followed as they both grabbed what they could and hurled it at each other. Soon, innocent bystanders got hit, and they retaliated until it seemed the entire cafeteria had joined in the fight.

Mr. Gunnoe blew into the microphone. It squealed back at him. Through cupped hands, he called for order.

****

The four walls of the camp director's office were decorated with odd shapes of mismatched paneling and several antlers of various sizes. A small window was the only break in the vertical sea of brown. A thin, white curtain hung crookedly over it. In front of the window sat a large, gray, metal desk covered with years of scars and coffee-cup rings. Mark and Joe sat on opposite sides of the desk in uncomfortable metal chairs. Both were adorned with bits of food from the fight.

If only I could talk to Whit, Mark thought. *He knows how Joe is. He won't let them punish me.*

Like an answered prayer, the door suddenly opened, and Whit walked in. Mark's heart leaped, not only because of the hope Whit always seemed to radiate, but also because it was the first time Mark had seen him in a week. Whit glanced at Joe, then Mark. The normal twinkle in his eyes was gone, and his bushy, white eyebrows pressed together into a frosty frown.

Oh no, Mark thought as his heart fell.

Whit pushed the door closed. The room was thick with his disapproval as he stroked his mustache for several moments. "I don't know what I'm going to do with you two," he finally said as he walked behind the desk. He didn't sound angry—not as he did the last time he scolded Mark for being disobedient—so Mark felt slightly relieved.

"You're the camp director?" Joe asked, astounded. A small piece of lettuce fell from his hair.

"For this week I am," he said, then hit the top of the desk with his hand. "I haven't had this kind of trouble with even our smallest kids—ever! What do you have to say for yourselves?"

"It was *his* fault!" Joe gestured at Mark.

Mark's mouth fell open. "That's a lie!"

Joe started to argue, but Whit held up his hand. "Quiet! Right now it doesn't matter who started it. The point is, it started. The point is, you two were responsible. So you can plan now to give the cafeteria a thorough scrubbing from top to bottom. Any more trouble and I'll put you both on kitchen cleanup for the rest of camp."

Joe looked as if he might say something, but he lowered his head. Mark and Whit made eye contact. Whit shook his head. For Mark, the disappointment was worse than the punishment.

Suddenly, they heard shouts from outside. The three of them turned to the window, where they saw people running past.

Whit wrenched open the window and shouted at a passerby, "What's going on?"

"The lake!" a young camper replied breathlessly. "Someone fell in by the old dock!"

Mark and Joe joined Whit at the window. "The old dock?" Whit asked with disbelief. It was as if he couldn't believe someone would dare step beyond all the warning signs there.

"Just look!" the camper said, pointing.

They did. Sure enough, people were running toward the dock, where a crowd had already gathered.

CHAPTER SIX

Nearly Fatal

Mark and Joe followed closely behind Whit as he made his way through the crowd. "What's going on? What happened?" Whit asked.

The scene they came upon answered everything. A very wet, very limp boy lay on the ground face down. David, also drenched, was feverishly pushing on the kid's back, trying to pump water out of him. A red ribbon of blood ran from a gash in the boy's forehead.

"Mouth to mouth!" Whit shouted as he dropped to his knees next to David and the boy.

They turned the boy onto his back and, with teamwork precision, applied their combined first-aid knowledge to help him. Each second moved like a minute. Mark wondered how long the boy could live without breathing.

Whit and David kept up their rhythm. They pumped his chest, counting in one-thousands, then breathed into him . . . then counted . . . then breathed.

"Lord, help us," Whit gasped.

How long has it been? Mark wondered.

Count . . . breathe . . .

Mark gazed at the boy's face and realized he had seen him earlier near the old dock. He was one of Joe's gang. Mark looked over at Joe, who watched Whit and David work with a stunned expression on his face.

"Stand back!" Whit shouted before descending on the boy's mouth again.

"Did anybody call an ambulance?" someone asked anxiously.

"I did," came the answer from the cowboy Mark had seen guiding horseback riders in the afternoon. "They're on the way."

"Go to the front driveway and wait for them, will you, Wes?" Whit said quickly.

Wes nodded and pushed his way through the crowd.

Suddenly the kid coughed, inhaled with a wheeze, then coughed again. Water spilled from his mouth. He gagged and coughed harder.

"That's it," Whit said softly as he turned him on his side. "Get it all out."

The kid retched and heaved for a couple of minutes. His breathing was labored, but at least he was breathing.

"Thank God," someone said. Gentle applause rippled through the crowd.

The boy opened his eyes long enough to say something about the dock being slippery, then passed out again. Whit turned his attention to the bleeding forehead.

"Good work," Whit said softly to David.

"I want a raise if I'm going to do this kind of work," David said with a smile.

"What happened?" Whit asked the crowd.

"He tried to walk out to the end of the dock," a young girl said. "I yelled at him to stop, but he wouldn't listen. Then I saw him fall in, and I ran and got Mr. Boyer."

It took a moment for Mark to remember that Mr. Boyer was David.

"It's a good thing you were nearby," Whit said to David.

David nodded. Mark saw him glance at Patti, whom Mark noticed for the first time standing opposite him in the crowd.

"David dove into the water to get him," Patti offered.

"Why was he out there?" Whit asked.

No one answered.

Mark looked over to see if Joe might say something, but he was gone. Mark quickly scanned the area and spotted him halfway across the field, headed for the cabins. He walked alone, his shoulders hunched, his head hung low.

Off in the distance, a siren wailed.

****

The boy—later identified as Brad Miller—was taken to the hospital. Whit followed in his own car. Mark looked back to the old dock and knew what had happened. Brad Miller took Joe's dare. He wanted to pass the initiation to be in Joe's gang. But why was Brad trying to walk to the end of the dock when Joe was with Mark in Whit's office?

"Did you see that?" Patti asked as she walked up behind Mark.

"Yeah," Mark said. "I saw it."

"He would've drowned out there if David hadn't rescued him."

Mark felt a wave of anger wash over him. Why did it seem as though everything centered on David? "I guess he's your big hero now," he said.

"He's *everybody's* hero," Patti replied. She was getting that tone in her voice again.

"He's not mine," Mark said.

"That's because you're jealous," Patti sneered.

"Whit saved Brad. David was only helping," Mark said stubbornly. "And I'm not jealous."

"There wouldn't have been a Brad to save if David hadn't pulled him out of the water first," Patti countered.

Mark didn't have an immediate response, so he simply folded his arms and grunted. After a brief pause, he replied,

"Sure, Patti. He's a big hero. Maybe they'll give him a medal."

"This is a waste of time," Patti said.

"It sure is," Mark agreed. "Why don't you go blow-dry his clothes or something?"

"It's more than I'd ever do for you!" she snapped.

"As if I care!" Mark retorted.

"You just wait. One of these days you'll read about yourself in my diary, and then you'll be ashamed!"

"Diary!"

"Yeah. And I'm going back to my cabin right now before I forget any of what happened. Especially what a jerk *you* are when *David* is such a hero."

Mark couldn't get over the statement that Patti kept a diary. "You really write in a diary?"

"Yeah. So what?"

"I just thought sissy girls wrote in diaries."

"Just goes to show what *you* know!" Patti said before marching off.

Mark watched her go. *I always knew having a girl as a friend couldn't work*, he thought.

CHAPTER SEVEN

Cleanup Duty

Mr. Gunnoe gave Mark a tour of the cafeteria and kitchen—mostly where the garbage bags and brooms could be found. Mark's cleanup duty was to start immediately.

"I don't know where your friend is," Mr. Gunnoe said, "but I'll be on the lookout for him. Avoiding the consequences only makes things worse in the long run."

Mark began to wipe off the tables.

Mr. Gunnoe watched for a moment, then said, "I guess Brad Miller is going to be kept overnight at the hospital for observation."

"Will he be all right?" Mark asked.

Mr. Gunnoe shrugged. "It seems that way. The doctors probably want to make sure he doesn't have a concussion.

That was a nasty cut on his head. Must've hit it on one of the beams when he fell. Really foolish being out there like that. Whit called from the hospital and said he wants anyone with information about why Brad was on the dock to talk to him."

Mark wondered where Joe was. *I'll bet he ran away*, Mark thought. *He knows he's going to be in big trouble.*

"Right now, nobody can figure it out, and the kid's not saying," Mr. Gunnoe said. "I sure hope this doesn't put a damper on the treasure hunt tomorrow."

"Treasure hunt?" Mark asked.

"Yeah! Don't you remember?"

Mark didn't.

"Oh, that's right. You just got here," Mr. Gunnoe recalled. "It's pretty simple. Teams of two are picked from the various cabins, and they follow clues from one point to another around the camp. The first to find the treasure wins it."

Mark finished cleaning off one table and started another. "What kind of treasure?"

Mr. Gunnoe looked as if no one had ever asked him that question before. "You know. A treasure. Gift certificates and goodies and . . . well, you know, a *treasure*."

Mark didn't know, but he decided not to press for a better answer.

The screen door at the end of the cafeteria slammed as Joe stepped in. "Janitor Joe at your service!" he announced, then popped a toothpick into his mouth.

"You're late!" barked Mr. Gunnoe.

"Yeah, too bad," Joe said as he sauntered between the tables toward them.

Joe's attitude was so confident that Mark was momentarily confused. *How can he act so cool? Doesn't he realize how much trouble he's going to be in?*

"You sweep up while Mark finishes the tables," said Mr. Gunnoe.

Joe grunted, grabbed a broom, and pushed it around without much enthusiasm. Mr. Gunnoe watched quietly until a phone rang somewhere in the kitchen. He left to answer it. Joe worked his broom around until he stood next to Mark.

"Too bad about that kid," Joe said, using his tongue to switch the toothpick from one side of his mouth to the other.

"His name is Brad," Mark said sharply. "You know that."

"I do?"

"You know you do," Mark said. "He was part of your gang."

Joe laughed and said, "You're out of your mind, Pressnot. What gang?"

"Your—" Mark then realized what kind of game Joe was playing. Mark also understood why Joe was being so cool. He probably threatened the other kids not to say anything. "You won't get away with it. Brad will tell."

Joe grinned as he said, "I guess that'll make it his word against mine."

Mark replied in a near whisper, "Brad's word and *mine*."

"Huh?"

"Remember? I was down at the old dock," Mark said. "I heard what you said to your gang."

Joe's toothpick twitched. "What are you talking about?"

"When you were behind the woodpile," Mark said. "I heard you dare them to walk to the end of the dock as part of an initiation into your gang."

Joe grabbed the handle of the broom so tightly that his knuckles turned white. "You're lying."

"I am not," Mark retorted. "And if you don't tell Mr. Whittaker why Brad was on the dock, I will."

The next thing happened so quickly that Mark wasn't sure until later what Joe did to him. All Mark knew then was that the wind got knocked out of him. He fell to the floor, clutching his stomach.

"What's going on here?" Mr. Gunnoe said, rushing up to them.

"It was an accident!" Mark heard Joe cry out. "I was sweeping and didn't see Mark behind me."

Mark gasped for air, his mouth opening and closing like a guppy at feeding time.

Mr. Gunnoe knelt next to him. "Take it easy, boy," he said. "Just calm down and breathe when your body's ready."

Mark saw spots in front of his eyes and rocked back and forth on the floor. He saw a drop of mashed potatoes under one of the tables.

"I guess it was the broom handle. It must've jabbed into him," Joe lied.

"Be more careful!" Mr. Gunnoe snapped as he eased Mark into a sitting position.

Mark groaned, making an unnatural sound somewhere in the back of his throat as he tried to take air in. His head spun.

"Go get some water," Mr. Gunnoe commanded.

Joe dropped the broom and obeyed.

"Don't move," Mr. Gunnoe said to Mark.

Moments later, when Joe returned with a glass of water, Mark was sitting on a chair, breathing painfully but more normally. Mr. Gunnoe took the glass of water from Joe and drank it. "Thanks," he said.

Mark started to speak, but Mr. Gunnoe stopped him. "Don't talk right now. Just close your eyes and take it easy."

"Yeah," Joe joined in. "Don't talk, Mark. You'll only make it worse for yourself if you say anything."

Mark looked up at Joe, who grinned at him wickedly.

CHAPTER EIGHT

A Chance Encounter

Mark lay on his bunk, his arm stretched over his eyes, while the cabin leader—a pimply-faced teenager named Terry—gave a little talk about helping others. "You know, Saint Paul said that sometimes we're the best people to help others, because we can show them the same kind of comfort that God showed us when *we* needed help. It's right here in Paul's second letter to the Corinthians . . ."

Mark's mind wasn't on Saint Paul or Second Corinthians, but on what to do about Joe. Jabbing him in the stomach with the broom handle was a low trick, even for Joe. And if he thought he was going to *scare* Mark into silence, he had another thing coming.

But Mark didn't say anything to Mr. Gunnoe about Joe's involvement with Brad or that Joe purposely hit him. Mr. Gunnoe wasn't the person to tell. Mark had to tell Whit. He was the only one who would understand or know what to do about it.

Mark glanced over at Joe's empty bunk. *I wonder where he is? Probably torturing other campers. How is he able to stay out later than everyone else and not get in trouble?* Mark rolled over onto his side. Terry was still talking about giving love and comfort to others, even those we don't like.

Mark shook his head. He couldn't imagine ever loving or giving comfort to Joe. He couldn't picture in his mind any time or place when he might care what happened to Joe. Joe was too much of a bully, too obnoxious. How could Mark feel anything other than hatred for him? Especially now that Joe was being *exceptionally* obnoxious.

Mark remembered that Patti had warned him about Joe when he first came to camp. She said Joe was acting worse than usual. *Why?* Mark mused. *What is it about camp that makes him act like a bigger bully than usual?*

Mark rolled over again and decided the reason didn't matter. Bullying kids was wrong—particularly when one nearly got killed just to be accepted by Joe and the rest of the gang. Whit needed to be told. And since Joe wouldn't tell him, Mark would have to.

Terry stopped talking and the heads of the other cabin

members turned as Mark climbed out of bed. He was still dressed, so all he had to do was put on his tennis shoes.

"What are you doing?" Terry asked.

Mark put on his shoes and brushed his dark hair away from his face. "I have to talk to Mr. Whittaker."

"I think you should wait until morning," said Terry.

"I can't," Mark replied as he strode to the door. "I have to talk to him now."

Mark didn't wait for Terry to answer. He stepped out onto the front porch of the cabin and let the screen door slam behind him. The night air was surprisingly chilly. He shivered slightly and walked toward the camp director's office. He guessed that Whit might have a bed near there.

The crickets chirped all around him as he walked up to the dark and apparently empty director's cabin. He knocked gently on the door, but no one answered. Where could Whit be? Mark knew he had returned from the hospital, so he had to be around the camp somewhere. Maybe Whit was making the rounds—just to make sure everyone was all right.

Except for the lights burning in the campers' cabins, where the evening devotions were being given and announcements were being made, the camp was deserted. A clear sky overhead gave everything a blue tint. Mark felt terribly alone. Once again, he was the outsider. He wondered where Patti was. *Not far from David, I'll bet.*

He walked around the main cabin, the dark cafeteria, the chapel, the storage building, the campers' cabins . . . but

Whit was nowhere to be found. Mark despaired of seeing him until morning when—*snap!*—he heard the sound of a branch breaking, probably under someone's foot. The crickets heard it, too, and stopped their singing.

Mark's guess was that the sound came from behind a small cabin on the edge of the woods. Unlike the others, no lights burned in its windows. It showed no signs of life at all. Yet he heard another sharp *snap* and knew it came from that direction.

He nearly called out Mr. Whittaker's name but stopped himself. He was afraid of drawing too much attention to himself. He figured he was already in enough trouble for walking out on Terry.

Maybe because he was so determined to find Whit, it didn't occur to Mark that the noise might *not* be Whit. He thought only that Mr. Whittaker was there doing whatever it was camp directors did at that time of night. So he crept along the side of the dark cabin and, at the last moment, decided to stop before stepping around the corner. Instead, he peeked around carefully.

Snap! came the sound again, and this time Mark could see that it wasn't Whit.

He got a bigger surprise than that.

Sitting on his haunches against the rear wall of the cabin, Joe Devlin stared into the black forest and absentmindedly snapped twigs in his hands. It was a peculiar scene for Mark to witness, because the moonlight struck Joe at just the right angle for Mark to see his face. His cheeks glistened. He was crying.

It surprised Mark so much that he wasn't sure what to do. There was Joe, his worst enemy in the world, completely alone and crying. For a fraction of a second, Mark wanted to step forward and make fun of him. *Look at you! Big, tough Joe Devlin crying like a little baby!* He wanted to shout it so the whole camp could hear and come out of their cabins to see for themselves that Joe wasn't to be feared.

But Mark couldn't do it. As much as he hated Joe, he couldn't wish on him the humiliation of being caught crying alone in the dark.

Snap.

Mark watched him and wondered why he was crying. Did he feel bad about what happened to Brad? Maybe he felt guilty. Maybe it was something else. Mark couldn't even guess. He simply stood and watched.

Joe suddenly looked in Mark's direction.

Mark retreated into the shadows. As he did, he bumped an old shutter leaning next to the cabin. It banged against the wall.

Joe jumped to his feet and wiped his face with his sleeve as he hissed, "Who's there? What do you want?"

Mark pressed himself against the wall, praying that the darkness covered him.

Joe took a step forward and squinted at the shadows. "Who's there?" he asked again, more nervously than before.

Mark feared that Joe would come investigate, but he

didn't. For reasons Mark would never know, Joe spun around and ran.

Mark breathed a sigh of relief, turned to leave . . . and ran straight into Terry.

"There you are," Terry said.

CHAPTER NINE

Trouble with the Treasure Hunt Teams

O nce again, Mark sat in one of the uncomfortable chairs in the camp director's office.

"May I *please* talk to Whit?" Mark asked.

Terry, now occupying the chair behind the desk, glared at Mark. "Whit had to go to Odyssey for the night. He'll be back tomorrow morning. If you had asked me instead of just running out in the middle of my Bible study, I could've told you that. What were you doing behind that cabin?"

"Looking for Whit," Mark answered simply.

"You thought Whit was hiding back" there?"

"I heard something and thought . . . " His voice trailed off as he realized how foolish any explanation would sound.

Why did he really think Whit would be wandering around behind a dark cabin?

"It could've been a bear," Terry said. "Or something worse. That's why we have rules in this camp, like staying in your cabin after dark. We don't want anyone to get hurt."

"I know," Mark said.

Terry eyed him suspiciously. "You were involved in that food fight earlier today, weren't you?"

Mark nodded and lowered his head.

"I thought so. Well, we have a *three-strikes-and-you're-out* policy here. You now have two strikes. One more and we'll send you home."

"Yes, sir," Mark said quietly.

Terry stood up to signal the end of their meeting. "Go straight back to the cabin and get to bed."

Mark stood, mumbled an apology, and left.

Once again, he thought as he walked across the compound, *Joe Devlin got me in trouble.*

When Mark finally got back to the cabin, he noticed that Joe was in his own bunk, fast asleep.

****

By morning, Mark had no idea of what to do about Joe. Part of him wanted to rush to Whit and explain everything. But the image of Joe sitting behind the cabin, crying, haunted him. It wasn't normal, Mark was sure. Kids only hide away and cry like that when something is terribly wrong.

Mark remembered when his parents first split up. He often sat alone in his room and listened to his favorite songs on a tape player . . . and cried.

To his own amazement, he decided to give Joe a break. *I'll give him one more chance to confess on his own*, Mark thought.

He sat down with his breakfast tray at a table in the cafeteria and eyed the food warily. He assumed he was looking at scrambled eggs, but they were a questionable shade of orange. He glanced around for Joe but didn't see him.

Patti arrived with her tray in hand. "Okay if I sit here?" she asked.

"If you want to," Mark replied. "But there's only one seat."

"That's all right," she said.

Mark asked her where David was.

"He's helping set up for the treasure hunt," she said before biting into a muffin.

"Oh." Mark picked up something he hoped was bacon.

"Mark, I wish we'd stop arguing so much," Patti said quickly.

Mark tilted his head in her direction. "I will if you will."

Patti sighed and said, "Truce."

"Truce," Mark agreed.

She pushed her tray away. "I . . . I miss talking to you about things."

"Me, too," Mark admitted. He suddenly realized he had never told her about his time with Whit before the trip to

Washington, D.C., or how his mom and dad were doing, or even what he knew about Joe Devlin and his gang. Sadly, he realized that if he couldn't talk to her, he couldn't talk to anyone.

"I like writing in my diary, but it's not the same," she added.

He perked up and suggested, "We could take a walk. We always talk our heads off when we walk." He actually looked forward to it. He could tell her everything that had happened.

"David likes to walk, too," she said.

David, Mark groaned inwardly. *Why do we always have to talk about him?*

"I've been wanting to tell you about him," she said, "because it's kind of serious now."

"Serious?"

She rubbed her nose nervously. "I like him in a way I've never liked anyone before. And he makes me feel things I've never felt before. That's why I've been acting kind of . . . "

"Weird?" Mark offered.

"Yeah, I guess," she conceded. "But I'm scared. Camp is going to end pretty soon, and . . . I don't know what's going to happen."

Mark didn't understand. "Happen? Like the camp might be bombed by terrorists or something?"

Patti ignored the question and turned to face him directly. "If you liked a girl and you were going to leave her to go home after a wonderful week together, would you write to her and be faithful to her?"

Mark looked around nervously. "Why do you have to ask me questions like that?"

"Because you're a boy," she said.

"But I'm not that kind of boy," he objected. "I don't care about stuff like that."

Patti persisted, "But do you think you'd at least kiss her good-bye?"

Mark groaned again and put his face in his hands. *I don't want to talk about this*, he thought.

"What's wrong?" she asked. "Is it wrong to want him to kiss me?"

"How should I know?" Mark answered, his voice full of irritation. "All I know is that they do it in the movies and I think it's gross, okay? Let's talk about something else."

"I *can't* talk about something else. This is what I keep thinking about. I can't eat, I can't sleep. I just think about him and get all goose-pimply."

Mark put his face in his hands again.

"I think I'm in love," she stated.

"I don't know anything about love," Mark said simply. "And I don't want to talk about this anymore."

"Why not?"

"I told you! I don't know anything about it. You may as well be talking about algebra or gabbing in a foreign language. I don't know, and I don't really care!"

Patti stood up and grabbed her tray. She wasn't angry. She merely looked at Mark with a sad expression on her face—as if she were about to leave for a faraway place and would never see him again.

Suddenly, Mark felt it was true. She was heading into new adventures, adventures he couldn't share because he wasn't ready. Niggling somewhere deep in that part of his heart that would one day grow to maturity, he realized this experience at camp wasn't something they would later shrug off. It was very real and very permanent, though neither of them knew why.

She walked away.

Mark opened his mouth to call after her, but then he closed it again. There wasn't really anything to say.

The public address system clicked on with a shrill whistle, and everyone turned to look at the front of the cafeteria. Whit, looking tired and disheveled in a gray "Camp What-a-Nut" jogging suit, smiled apologetically. "Excuse me," he said, then adjusted a few knobs on the control panel to get his voice to the right volume. After a moment of fiddling, he asked, "Can you hear me?"

Everyone shouted yes as one voice, and he laughed at the sound of it. It was good for Mark to hear Whit laugh. It seemed as though it had been a long time.

"Are you excited about the treasure hunt today?" he asked.

Again the cafeteria echoed with enthusiastic shouts.

He waved a long sheet of paper at them. "Good, because I'm now going to announce the pairings for the teams!"

A hush fell on the crowd as he proceeded down the list, cabin by cabin, team by team. Sometimes the announced pairings were greeted with laughter, other times with grumbles. When Whit reached Cabin Wabana, Mark sat up.

Mark didn't know his cabin mates very well, but he looked forward to the excitement of the hunt: figuring out the clues, beating the other teams, finding the treasure. *It might be the best thing about this camp*, Mark thought. He looked around eagerly to see whom he might recognize from his cabin.

Whit continued reading the names. "Cameron, Arnold . . . you're with Bob Martinez."

Hoots and howls came from the back of the cafeteria.

Since the list was alphabetically arranged, Whit called out "Devlin, Joe" next. Mark sat up in his seat as high as he could to get a look at who would be stuck with Joe. He turned his head right and left, wanting to catch that first look of surprise when the unknown victim's name was announced. He spotted Joe leaning casually against a side wall.

"Joe Devlin, you're paired with . . . " Whit peered over the sheet of paper, scanned the crowd, and said, "Mark Prescott."

CHAPTER TEN

First Clues

"**P**lease, Whit. You *can't* team me up with Joe!" Mark pleaded. He had rushed to get to Whit, nearly knocking people over as he pushed against the stream of campers leaving the cafeteria.

"*I* didn't team you up," Whit said. "That's just the way it worked out. And if I switch you around, I'll have to do it for anyone else who asks. I can't do that. You'll have to make the best of the situation."

"But you don't understand," Mark began to say, but he was interrupted by Joe's arrival.

"Well, ain't this an interesting turn of events," Joe sneered. "Me and Pressnot—together at last. It's a good thing I didn't have high hopes of finding the treasure."

Whit pushed some papers under his clipboard. "Frankly, I think this is the best thing that could happen to either of you. Working as a team toward a common goal will be a good lesson. That's the reason we're doing this treasure hunt."

"It's not fair!" Mark protested.

Whit smiled at him and answered, "Few things are."

"But you don't know about Joe," Mark began, his voice sounding shrill.

"What about Joe?" Whit asked.

"Yeah, what about me?" Joe repeated.

Mark was ready to confess everything he knew about Brad Miller and what had happened on the old dock. Then Whit would keep Joe from taking part in the treasure hunt, and Mark would get a new teammate. He looked at Whit, who watched him closely.

Mark coughed nervously and glanced at Joe's expressionless face—the sharp eyes, the high cheekbones. And Mark once again saw Joe's tears glistening in the moonlight. *Kids only hide away and cry like that when something is terribly wrong*, Mark remembered thinking.

"Well?" Whit prompted.

"He'll be a terrible teammate," Mark answered feebly.

Whit tucked his clipboard under his arm. "Case closed. Come on. Everyone's meeting under the flagpole."

****

"The rules are simple," Whit called out to the assembled campers. "Each team should have a sealed envelope. Does everyone have one?" He held up a sample envelope and looked around.

Mark glanced at Joe, who had the crushed envelope in his fist.

Whit continued, "When I fire the starting pistol, you'll open your envelopes for the first clue. If you can figure it out, that clue will tell you where to find the second clue. There are twelve clues in all, and the team that figures them all out should be able to find the treasure. Of course, first team to the treasure wins it. Any questions?"

The air was tense with excitement as Whit looked over the crowd. Mr. Gunnoe stepped forward. "Please don't throw the envelopes on the ground," he said. "You'll be immediately disqualified if you do."

Again Mark looked at Joe. He smirked back at Mark and pretended to puff on his toothpick as if it were a cigarette.

"Is everybody ready?"

The crowd roared *yes*.

Whit raised the starting pistol. "Then on your marks, get set . . . " He pulled the trigger, and the pistol popped loudly.

A mad scramble and commotion of tearing paper ensued as the teams opened their envelopes. Joe adroitly tore off the top of theirs and pulled out the sheet of paper inside. He held it up and away from Mark.

"What does it say?" Mark asked impatiently as he tried to get a look.

Joe thrust the paper at Mark. It said:

Long box of tin where food for thought
Might get you sustenance, cold and hot.

"Food for thought?" Joe asked. "Does the camp have a library?"

"Sustenance, cold and hot," Mark pondered. "The cafeteria!"

"That's too obvious," Joe argued. "The cold and hot might be talking about the utility shed where the water heaters are kept. It's made out of tin."

Mark watched as most of the other teams raced to the cafeteria. He pointed after them. "See, Joe? The cafeteria looks like it's made of tin, and it's long. Let's go!"

They argued the entire way to the cafeteria. Even when they found the second clue posted on a large sign there, Joe wouldn't admit that Mark was right. He simply grunted and said, "Don't let it go to your head, Pressnot."

Mark ignored him and looked up at the sign. It read:

If you yell these words, they'll make you hoarse,
But the four-legged kind is much better, of course.

"The stable!" Mark whispered to Joe, not wanting the other campers to hear.

"No way," Joe snapped. "That's too obvious."

Mark growled, "That's what you said about the cafeteria. Maybe the clues are easy at first and then get harder."

"Maybe not," Joe said stubbornly.

Once again, the sight of everyone else running to the stables was the only thing that persuaded Joe to go.

Once again, Mark wished Joe would fall off the face of the earth.

CHAPTER ELEVEN

So Much for Teamwork

Mark was right. The early clues were easy enough, but they grew increasingly difficult. And as the clues got harder, Joe and Mark argued more fiercely. Sometimes Mark came up with the answer, other times Joe did. The "who was right and who was wrong" count was close enough to keep either of them from insisting on having his own way. After a particularly nasty quarrel about clue number six, Mark wondered if any of the other teams came as near to physical blows as he and Joe did.

If this is a lesson about teamwork, then I'm not learning very much, Mark thought.

Fortunately, the other teams were equally baffled about the clues. Within an hour, pairs of campers were spread out all over the greater Camp What-a-Nut area as the teams chased after their guesses. Mark imagined that they would look like maniacal ants if someone could see them from above.

Whit had to rescue one camper from the top of a tree. It was then that Whit made the rounds to assure the teams that clues weren't hidden in any place that might hurt them.

Mark and Joe ran to the dugout by the oldest baseball field at the farthest point from the camp, where Mark was sure they would find the ninth clue. It was there, hanging on a crudely painted sign.

"Told you so," Mark said.

"Shut up," Joe retorted. "I'm trying to concentrate."

Mark looked around. As best as he could tell, they were the first ones to find the clue.

The sign said:

A shelter in a storm, a haven to protect,
The next clue can be found with the deepest respect.

Mark read it again but couldn't figure out what it was talking about.

Suddenly Joe laughed. It startled Mark, because he couldn't remember Joe ever laughing, except when he'd just done something cruel to someone. "This one's easy," Joe said.

"Where is it?" Mark asked.

"Can't you guess?" Joe taunted.

"No, Joe. Don't waste time."

"Shelter . . . protect . . . deepest . . . " Joe hung the words out for Mark to consider.

Mark put his hands on his hips, then jerked at his sagging jeans. "If you know the answer, tell me. I don't know."

"The bomb shelter," Joe said.

Mark shrugged. "What bomb shelter?"

Joe nodded toward the lake. "If you follow the shore around to the other side of those trees, there's an abandoned bomb shelter."

"Why would anybody put a bomb shelter back there?" Mark challenged.

"Because there's an old, burned-out house back there, too. Maybe the owner was afraid of bombs," Joe said as he started to walk away.

"I think you're wrong," Mark said.

Joe shrugged and said, "Stay behind if you want."

Mark followed, though it didn't make much sense to him.

The layout was exactly as Joe said. The shore of the lake wound around and disappeared behind a part of the forest that reached down to the water. From the camp, Mark never would've suspected it went on so far.

"How do you know about the bomb shelter?" Mark asked.

Joe chuckled but didn't answer.

They had to trudge through a tangle of wild branches and bushes, some lashing at their arms and legs, until they came to the shell of an old house. It was nestled in the woods and was clearly the casualty of a fire, perhaps long ago. Mark guessed that it belonged to someone who worked with the camp itself. Why it wasn't restored after the fire was any-body's guess.

"The shelter is over there," Joe said, leading the way to the side of the house. Mark stayed a few steps behind.

The place was so desolate and distant from the camp that Mark felt sure they were making a mistake. Why would Whit choose such a remote place to hide a clue?

Joe stopped at the edge of a rectangular hole in the ground. A short stairwell led to a large, steel door at the bottom. The door reminded Mark of the entrance to a bank vault. "The clue must be inside," Joe said as he descended the stairs.

"This doesn't make sense, Joe," said Mark at the top of the stairs. "Whit said he wouldn't hide the clues anywhere dangerous."

"This isn't dangerous," Joe said with a scowl. "I've been in here plenty of times. Don't be such a baby."

"But . . . where is everybody else?"

Joe pushed at the steel door and spoke between grunts. "You said yourself the clues got harder. Obviously, bright boy, we were the first ones to figure it out. Give me a hand."

Mark hesitantly joined Joe at the bottom of the stairs and pushed. The door suddenly gave with a rusty, wrenching sound.

"Nasty, huh?" Joe reached down and grabbed a broken cin-der block. "You gotta prop it open or it'll swing shut again."

"I don't like this," Mark said nervously.

"Do you wanna win the treasure or not?" Joe asked as he stepped into the darkness.

"They wouldn't put the clue in the dark," Mark observed.

"Maybe they had a light in here and it went out. You can't expect them to think of everything," Joe growled. He lit a match and added, "I'm telling you it's in here."

"Where'd you get the matches?" asked Mark.

Joe held the match high. "I always carry matches," he said. "You never know when you'll need 'em. There. That's what I was looking for."

Mark brightened. "The clue?"

"Nah," Joe replied with a chuckle, "a candle I found in here the other night."

Mark looked around, taking in as much as he could by the light of Joe's candle. Apart from being cold and damp, the bomb shelter was in a state of disarray. Shelves along the walls were broken or hanging loosely at odd angles. Mark noticed a couple of dented cans of food on one shelf and several others that had dropped onto the floor. In the center, a table, tilted from a broken leg, was surrounded by tipped-over chairs—like pins that had been clobbered by a large bowling ball. Two cots with mildewed cushions rested against a side wall.

The scene was a crumbling version of a picture he had once seen in history class. He remembered it from his text-book—a black-and-white photo of a bomb shelter built in the 1950s, when many Americans were afraid the Russians might drop an atomic bomb on them. Mark's uneasiness grew to genuine fear.

"There's no clue in here. Let's go," Mark said.

"Is little Marky scared?" Joe teased.

"I'm going," Mark said as he turned toward the door.

Joe laughed and grabbed Mark's arm. "Don't leave me, Marky! I'm afraid of the dark!"

"Stop it!" Mark jerked his arm away and lost his balance. He clawed at the air for something to grab onto, but nothing was there. His leg lashed out and connected with the cinder block that held the door. He stumbled against the wall and slid to the ground.

"Ouch," Joe said. "Marky fall down and go boom. Is Marky going to cry now?"

Mark leaped angrily to his feet. "I've had enough of you, Joe!" he shouted as he moved toward him with clenched fists.

Joe snickered scornfully and lifted his own fists to defend himself. Suddenly his expression—so confident and defiant—twisted into one of alarm. "The door!" he cried.

Mark thought it was some sort of trick and didn't look.

Joe sprang past Mark, his arms reaching out. The door slammed shut; the bang of steel against the frame rang in Mark's ears. It was solid and final.

Joe was on his knees, frantically clawing at a door handle that wasn't there. Mark saw it sitting uselessly in a cobwebbed corner.

"Help me!" Joe shouted as he dug his fingers into the thin

line between the door and the frame. Mark rushed over and did the same at a higher point. It was no use.

They were trapped.

CHAPTER TWELVE

The Shelter

Since neither of them had a watch, Mark wasn't sure how long they spent trying to find a tool, a blade, a thin piece of wood—anything that might fit between the door and the jamb so they could force the door open again. No success.

After that, they pounded on the door and screamed for help. But they heard only the dead silence of the enclosed room.

Mark remembered another tidbit from his history class: the bomb shelters were generally built airtight, with their own air purifiers to keep radioactive air out. He mentioned it to Joe.

"What does that mean?" Joe asked.

"It means we may not have air for very long," Mark answered.

"Then what are we gonna do?"

"I don't know."

"Great. Just great," Joe said spitefully. "We'll be stuck here forever because you didn't watch where you were going."

"What! I lost my balance because you grabbed my arm!" Mark shouted. "It was your idea to come here in the first place, don't forget. I knew it was wrong."

"I just followed the clue," Joe insisted.

"Yeah, sure. Real smart. Everyone else is digging up the treasure somewhere else while we're stuck in here—because *you're* Mr. Brain Boy who followed the clue," Mark sneered.

"Shut your mouth, Pressnot!" Joe said as he jumped on Mark. They fell to the ground in a tangle of flailing arms and legs, grunts and groans, hits and misses. They rolled into the table and knocked the candle over. It went out.

Unable to see each other, they separated. Mark peered into the thick blackness. It was so dark, in fact, that he couldn't even see his own hand in front of his face. "What happened?"

"You knocked the candle over!" Joe cried out.

Mark tried to sit up but hit his head on the bottom of the table. "Ouch!" he moaned.

"Where is it?" Joe asked.

Mark reached up and felt the rough, splintered edge of the table top. His fingers crawled along the surface until they connected with warm wax. He grabbed it. "Here it is!"

Mark could hear Joe fumbling in the darkness. "I can't

find my matches," he said and fumbled around some more. "I can't find them! They must've fallen out of my pocket while I was beating you up."

"You weren't beating me up," Mark muttered.

Joe shuffled around, rubbing his hands against the ground. "Help me find them!"

They crawled on their hands and knees around the shelter floor. The swirling dust made them cough, and the darkness made them bump into each other several times. Mark realized how dangerous their predicament was when something scratched his arm. He screamed.

"What's the matter?" Joe shouted.

"Something scratched my arm."

"Like what?"

"I don't know!" Mark said, rubbing his arm.

"It wasn't a rat, was it?" Joe asked, panicked.

"I said I don't know!" Mark was annoyed.

"I hate rats!" Joe cried out. "Don't move."

They sat still for a moment, listening in the darkness for any telltale signs of life. Nothing happened.

"Okay," Joe said.

They renewed their search for the matches.

"I found them!" Joe shouted after several minutes. Again, Mark could hear him rustling in the dark. There was a sharp scratching sound, followed by a spark and dim flame of the match. "Oh, no. This is my last match."

"Be careful," Mark said as they found the candle again and lit it.

Even in the yellow glow, Mark was glad to see Joe's face. He leaned back and realized what had scratched him earlier. Certainly not a rat. It was a nail sticking out of a fallen shelf.

"You're gonna get lockjaw now," Joe stated.

"I will not," Mark replied as he checked his arm. "It's only a little scratch. It didn't even draw blood."

"It doesn't have to draw blood to give you lockjaw," said Joe. And they spent the next several minutes arguing about the causes and cures of lockjaw.

About the time that Joe was saying Mark would need 17 vaccinations with 12-inch-long needles, the candle hissed and flickered.

"We shouldn't talk so much," Mark said. "I think the candle is flickering because we're running out of air."

They sat in silence, each thinking his own thoughts. Joe's breathing was thick and hard. Somehow it made the solitude more unbearable, so Mark said, "They'll realize we're missing and come look for us. I wonder who else knows about this place?"

Joe shook his head. "Nobody," he said.

"How did *you* find out about it?"

"The old man in the stables told me about it," he responded. "We're pals. He said it was a big secret."

"Great. So nobody else knows about it except the old man."

Joe shrugged and said, "Guess not."

Mark said carefully, "Joe, if it's such a big secret, why did you think Whit would use it as part of the treasure hunt?"

Joe was silent for a moment. "I didn't think of that," he finally replied.

Mark groaned and lowered his head onto his arms.

"I thought it'd be a neat hideout for the gang," Joe said, looking around proudly as if he were seeing the shelter for the first time.

"Your gang," Mark said disdainfully. "They're nothing but trouble."

Joe sat straight up and glared at Mark. "Don't you talk about my gang like that."

"Tell me one good thing any gang of yours ever did," Mark challenged him.

"They do lots of good things!" Joe said. "For me."

"I'll bet Brad Miller would argue that," Mark mumbled.

Joe cocked his head. "What did you say?" he demanded.

"Nothing," Mark said.

But it was clear that Joe heard Mark's comment, because he said softly, "I didn't mean for Brad to get hurt. He was supposed to walk on the dock when the whole gang was there— later on. He wasn't supposed to go out there by himself."

"Why did he have to go out at all?" Mark asked.

"For the initiation! If you knew anything about gangs, you wouldn't ask such dumb questions."

"Why do you have to have initiations?" Mark persisted.

"Because . . . " Joe began, then realized he didn't have a proper defense. "Because that's how gangs are formed."

Joe spread his arms and continued, "I wasn't gonna make him walk the dock. I just wanted to see if he'd do it. I didn't know he was gonna do something so stupid as to walk it alone. Okay?" His voice trembled, and he quickly looked away.

"I still don't get why—" Mark started.

Joe jerked his head around to face Mark. "I don't wanna talk about it. Say another word and I'll pound you good and hard."

Mark frowned and said, "Yeah, that's your answer for everything, isn't it? You'll pound me. We're gonna die in here, and you wanna pound me. Why do you have to be such a creep?"

"Shut up," Joe said.

"In Odyssey—and here," Mark continued. "Why do you have to be like that? Why've you been so nasty all week?"

"I said to shut up!" Joe yelled, throwing himself at Mark. Again they rolled around on the floor as each one tried to get on top. Again they rolled once too far and banged the table. Again the candle tipped and fell over, going out. The darkness swallowed them.

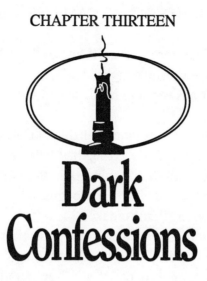

CHAPTER THIRTEEN

Dark Confessions

They sat in silence in the darkness. Mark didn't think there was anything else to do. He considered crawling around to look for the candle until he remembered Joe was out of matches anyway. So he sat still. Once or twice, he prayed for God to help them find a way out.

"Help!" Joe suddenly screamed at the top of his lungs, startling Mark. "Help! Help!"

"Joe!" Mark said loudly, trying to be heard above the scream.

"Help! Help! Hellllppp!" He kept screaming until Mark had to put his hands over his ears. Joe's voice eventually went hoarse.

"They'll look for us. They'll find us," Mark said desperately when Joe was quiet again.

Joe didn't answer, and Mark settled into the stillness of surrender.

Mark shifted his position, realizing too late that he'd been sitting cross-legged. His left leg had fallen asleep. He carefully stretched it out and winced as the pins and needles danced up and down his thigh. He groaned.

"What's wrong?" Joe croaked.

"My leg fell asleep," answered Mark. He rubbed it for a moment, then said, "I wish I could stand up."

"Ha. I wish we were out of here," Joe snorted.

"I wish we were out of here and back in Odyssey," Mark amended. "I wanna be back home, in my own bed, in my own room."

Joe murmured, "At least you have a home."

Mark was puzzled by the statement. Joe had a home. Mark had been there once when he was accused of slashing one of Joe's bike tires. Joe had a father who was a barber, a mother who stayed at home, and a younger brother who was a general nuisance.

The more Mark thought about it, the more he remembered his impression at the time that Joe's home wasn't a happy one. He felt sorry for Joe then, much as he had felt sorry for Joe when he saw him crying behind the cabin. He thought of how the moonlight hit Joe's face in just such a way to show the tears on his cheeks. Even now, he could hear the sniffling.

Mark sat up. The sniffling wasn't in his memory. It was real. Somewhere in the darkness, Joe was crying.

Mark cleared his throat and said, "We'll get out of here, Joe."

Joe didn't reply. The sniffles turned to sobs. The sobs turned to a mournful cry.

The sound tugged at Mark's heart. He felt a mixture of feelings. On the one hand, he couldn't listen to such sounds in pitch black without wanting to cry himself. He feared that Joe was crying because he knew they were truly trapped and were going to die. What else was left to do?

On the other hand, Mark felt a twinge of curiosity. He wanted to *see* Joe cry. He wanted to study it as one might study a peculiar freak of nature.

Mark didn't know what to do or say. It wasn't like the encounter behind the cabin, where Joe would have been mortified to be seen by Mark. Here, Joe was crying openly. There were no secrets in such a tiny place.

He shuffled uneasily. *Do something. Say something,* he told himself. But he froze with the fear of doing or saying something stupid. He was clumsy when it came to other people's emotions. He remembered nights when his mother sat at the kitchen table and cried because of her problems with his dad. Mark never knew what to say to her. Sometimes he made her a cup of tea and slipped away to another room so she could cry in private. Other times, he just sat and held her hand. But there was no tea to be made here, and he wouldn't dare hold Joe's hand.

He took a deep breath and offered up a tiny prayer, asking God to help him. "They'll find us, Joe," Mark said as reassuringly as he knew how.

"I don't care," Joe sobbed.

Mark closed his eyes, as if it made a difference in that darkness. "You don't care if they find us?"

"No," Joe said.

Maybe all that screaming made him lose his mind, Mark thought. "Why don't you care?"

Joe fell silent again.

Mark thought through all the reasons Joe might not want to be rescued. "Are you afraid of getting in trouble because of what happened to Brad?" Mark finally asked, choosing the only reason that seemed to make sense.

"No." He sniffled and went quiet again.

Mark waited, wondering if he should come up with another idea. Just as he opened his mouth to speak, Joe said, "It's what I said before."

Mark didn't remember what Joe had said before.

"About home," Joe explained, as if he knew Mark didn't remember.

"What happened at home?" Mark asked gently. He was suddenly unsure of whether he really wanted to know, but he figured he should follow this to its end.

"My mom and dad," Joe started to say, then got choked up

again. He coughed and took a deep breath. "My dad moved out last week, and I think they're going to get a divorce."

Mark looked into the blackness, trying to form the words to say. "I'm sorry," he finally managed.

"I don't want you to feel sorry!" Joe snapped. "It's none of your business anyway!"

Mark normally would have agreed. It wasn't any of his business. Joe was a bully who drove him crazy. Why should he say any more? Why should he listen to his problems? Not long ago, he even told himself he hated Joe. *It's none of my business*, Mark thought.

But he knew in his heart that wasn't true. It *was* his business. It was his business because his own father had left him, and he knew how that felt.

Then Mark heard the voice of a pimply-faced teenager named Terry echoing in his head from the night before. "Saint Paul said that sometimes we're the best people to help others because we can show them the same kind of comfort that God showed us when *we* needed help. It's right here in Paul's second letter to the Corinthians . . ."

Mark shuffled in place uneasily. For the first time since he met Joe, he had something in common with him.

"Look, Joe, I know how you feel," Mark whispered. "My parents split up, too, you know."

Mark imagined that Joe nodded in response.

He went on, "It hurt a lot when my dad left. I thought it was the end of the world. In a way I guess it was, because we moved here right after that. All I kept thinking was that I wanted them to get back together."

"Hm," Joe said.

"And I figured it was all my fault. I figured my dad left because maybe I did something wrong or maybe I didn't do enough of something or maybe I didn't do anything at all."

"I've done plenty," Joe remarked.

Mark was sure he had, but he continued anyway. "I figured out that grownups pretty much do what they want without talking to kids."

"You're telling me!" Joe said.

"I learned that my dad didn't leave because of me. It didn't have anything to do with me. He left because of things I couldn't understand."

"Why didn't he tell me that?" Joe complained. "He could've said something to us. Doesn't he care?"

"He cares. He just isn't thinking about it right now. Didn't you ever run away without telling anybody why you were leaving or where you were going?"

Joe was quiet for a moment. "Yeah, a couple of times."

"In a way, your dad's doing the same thing," Mark said. "Except you can't chase after him or make him come back."

"Then what are we supposed to do? My mom's a wreck, and my little brother walks around the house crying all the time."

"You'll have to do what I did, I guess. Just wait and see what happens, 'cause things keep changing whether we want them to or not. All we can do is hang on. Even when you don't feel like it, you have to hang on."

Mark peered into the darkness, glad for it now because he knew Joe's face would have stopped him from saying any more. He added, "See, it's not what happens to us, it's how we react to what happens to us."

Thanks, Whit, Mark thought.

"Yeah? Well, what do you know about it?" Joe said abruptly, as if he'd decided he appeared foolish taking advice from Mark.

Mark didn't get the chance to answer. A sound caught his attention that was unlike anything he'd heard for quite a while. It wasn't the numbing drone of the enclosed shelter or Joe's thick breathing, or even the ringing in his own ears. He thought he heard voices.

"What's that?" Joe whispered.

Before either of them could move or say anything, the door was pushed open.

"In here," a voice said.

"It's so dark," said a higher voice Mark recognized.

"I'll turn on the flashlight. It's a great place. You'll like it," the first voice said.

A blinding light washed out the darkness and Mark's ability to see anything. But he didn't need to. He knew who his rescuers were—Patti and David.

CHAPTER FOURTEEN

An Accidental Rescue

"**W**hat do you mean nobody's looking for us?" Joe asked indignantly after Mark explained to Patti and David what they'd been through.

"Everybody's still on the treasure hunt. Why would they think you were missing?" David asked.

"I don't believe it," Joe groaned.

"How long have we been in here? What time is it?" Mark asked.

Patti glanced at her watch. "It's 11:30."

"No way!" Joe shouted.

Mark was amazed. "We've only been in here for an hour and a half?"

Patti giggled and said, "What did you think, you were in here for a whole day or something?"

"What are you doing here anyway?" David asked, taking charge. "This area is off-limits."

"I didn't know that," Mark replied.

"What are *you two* doing here if it's off-limits?" Joe asked coyly.

Patti blushed, and David was briefly flustered. "We . . . we were making the rounds . . . checking things out."

Joe and Mark looked at each other knowingly.

"What about you?" Patti countered to Joe. "What're those streaks on your face? Were you crying?"

"Get out of my way." Joe suddenly pushed past them and stomped up the stairs that led away from the shelter.

Mark lingered for a moment as David and Patti looked at one another awkwardly. "I guess I could use some fresh air," Mark said.

"Somebody should seal this shelter up," David suggested. Mark walked away from them toward the stairs and hesitated at the top.

"Let me see what it looks like first," he heard Patti insist from below.

"I can't *now*," David said sternly. "We have to go back to the camp"—his volume increased as if he was speaking for Mark's benefit—"now that we've finished our rounds."

"Oh. Okay," Patti said, defeated.

As the three of them made their way back to camp, Mark

wondered if he had ruined Patti's chance to get that good-bye kiss from David. Judging from the sour expression on her face, Mark was sure he had.

****

Back at Camp What-a-Nut, the treasure hunt had just finished. A team from a girl's cabin called Gitchy-Goomy solved the clues that finally led to the Wabana cabin, where the treasure was hidden. They screamed as they opened the box and found gift certificates for free ice cream at Whit's End.

The box was hidden under Mark's bunk.

"Hello, Mark," Mr. Gunnoe said as Mark turned from the crowd.

"Hi."

"Exciting, isn't it?" said Mr. Gunnoe. "I suppose you didn't expect the treasure to be hidden under your bunk."

Mark shook his head no, then asked, "Do you know what the answer to the ninth clue was?" The ninth clue was the one that had sent Mark and Joe on the wild goose chase to the bomb shelter.

Mr. Gunnoe thoughtfully tapped his chin with his finger. "The ninth clue? Oh, yes. That's the one that said, *'A shelter in a storm, a haven to protect; the next clue can be found with the deepest respect.'*"

Mark nodded again.

"I would've thought it was obvious," Mr. Gunnoe said

with a chuckle. "The answer was the camp *chapel*. A shelter in a storm, a haven to protect, a place of deep respect . . . rather poetic, I think. What did you think the answer was?"

"I don't want to talk about it." Mark frowned and strolled away. He headed across the compound toward the cafeteria. More than anything, he wanted a tall glass of lemonade to soothe his parched throat.

On the way, he saw Whit in the distance, talking to David and Patti. Whit shook a finger at them sternly, then spun on his heel and strode in the opposite direction. David and Patti had a brief discussion, then went their separate ways.

Uh oh, Mark thought.

Patti marched toward Mark, then scowled when she saw it was him. "Thanks a lot," she snapped.

"What's wrong?"

"We told Whit about what happened to you and Joe in the shelter. We figured he'd be happy with us because we rescued you."

"He wasn't happy?"

Patti's brow wrinkled into a deep frown. "Yeah, he was happy we found you. But he was mad because me and David were down there at all. He said David knew the shelter was off-limits. Especially for a boy and a girl alone. He said we had no business being there."

"He's right, isn't he?"

Patti glared at Mark. "Of course he's right. He's *always* right. But that doesn't make me feel better."

Mark simply shrugged and said, "Thanks for rescuing us anyway."

Patti grunted and stormed off.

Mark continued toward the cafeteria and spotted Joe under a nearby tree. Joe was surrounded by his gang. It was clear to Mark that he was telling a very inflated account of their adventure in the bomb shelter. "We dug ourselves out with our bare hands!" Mark heard him say.

Mark grimaced and shook his head. Then, just as he reached for the door to the cafeteria, he felt a tap on his shoulder. He turned to find himself face to face with Joe.

"Hey, Pressnot," Joe said, his face now scrubbed to cover any hint that he'd been crying.

"Yeah?"

"Well . . . you know," he said.

"Huh?"

"*You know,*" Joe insisted.

Mark said that he didn't.

Joe shuffled his feet and frowned. "Just make me say it, why don't you?" he said.

"Make you say *what?*" Mark asked.

"Make me say . . . well, thanks."

Mark shrugged and said, "I didn't do anything."

"Maybe you did, maybe you didn't," Joe said. "And maybe I can do you a favor sometime."

Mark looked at Joe thoughtfully. "You can do me a favor now," he said.

Joe raised an eyebrow. "Yeah? Like what?"

"Tell Whit what happened to Brad Miller."

Joe cringed. "You're kidding."

"Nope." Mark shook his head. "Tell him."

Joe looked down at his dirty tennis shoes for a moment, then sighed and said, "We'll see."

"And one more thing," Mark added.

"Yeah?"

"Stop calling me Pressnot." Mark then walked into the cafeteria, where he found an ice-cold glass of lemonade.

Epilogue

O n Saturday morning, campers piled into buses and cars to go back to their homes. Whit kindly gave Mark a lift to save his mom the trouble of coming all the way to camp to get him.

Whit navigated the car beyond the bumpy dirt road that led away from the camp and settled into the smoother main road to Odyssey. Then he spoke. "A curious thing happened last night," he said.

Mark looked up at Whit's round face—cheerily adorned with tufts of white hair on top, above his eyes, and below his nose.

Whit continued, "Joe Devlin showed up at my cabin and said he needed to talk to me."

Mark sat up expectantly.

"He said he had an anonymous tip about why Brad Miller was out on the old dock," Whit said.

Mark squirmed in his seat. "An anonymous tip?"

"Uh huh." Whit nodded. "He said that Brad Miller was out there as part of an initiation to get into a gang. But Joe wasn't sure what gang."

Mark folded his arms and scowled. *That Joe*, he thought. *A creep to the very end.*

Whit smiled and said, "It doesn't matter. When Brad realized he wasn't going back to camp—and wouldn't have to face Joe—he told us everything."

"Will Joe get in trouble?" Mark asked.

"I doubt it. Officially speaking, he didn't do anything wrong. He didn't *force* Brad to go out on the dock. But *unofficially* . . . I think I'll have a little talk with him."

Mark grinned and sat back in the passenger's seat. *Sooner or later, everybody gets what's coming to him,* Mark thought.

Later, as they drew to a stop in Mark's driveway, Whit said, "You know that I wasn't at camp the other night."

"Terry said you had business in Odyssey—or something like that," Mark said as he pulled his bag from the backseat.

"Something like that," Whit said. "I got to talking to a man and woman—a married couple—and time slipped away from us. Seems like we talked most of the night, in fact. Just trying to sort things out. I think we did."

Mark looked Whit full in the face, trying to figure out why he was telling him about it.

Whit beamed and said, "Go on, Mark. I'll see you later."

Mark closed the car door and stepped away as Whit backed out of the driveway. The screen door creaked open. Mark waved as Julie stepped out. "Hi, Mom!"

Then Richard followed her.

Mark suddenly remembered Whit's words. *Seems we talked most of the night, in fact. Just trying to sort things out. I think we did.*

Mark dropped his bag and ran to his mother and father. The three of them collided into a crushing hug. Mark could hardly speak, afraid to ask the question, then asking it anyway: "What are you doing here, Dad?"

He smiled and said, "We're getting back together."

Mark looked from his mother's face and back to his father's with disbelief. "What?"

"I know you've been waiting a long time," Richard said. "We're finally going to be a family again."

About the Author

Paul McCusker is producer, writer, and director for the *Adventures in Odyssey* audio series. He is also the author of a variety of popular plays including *The First Church of Pete's Garage*, *Snapshots & Portraits*, and co-author of *Sixty-Second Skits* (with Chuck Bolte).

Other Works by the Author

NOVELS:
>
> Strange Journey Back (Focus on the Family)
> High Flyer with a Flat Tire (Focus on the Family)
> The Secret Cave of Robinwood (Focus on the Family)
> Behind the Locked Door (Focus on the Family)

INSTRUCTIONAL:
>
> Youth Ministry Comedy & Drama:
> Better Than Bathrobes But Not Quite Broadway
>> (with Chuck Bolte; Group Books)

PLAYS:
>
> Pap's Place (Lillenas)
> A Work in Progress (Lillenas)
> Snapshots & Portraits (Lillenas)
> Camp W (Contemporary Drama Services)
> Family Outings (Lillenas)
> The Revised Standard Version of Jack Hill (Baker's Plays)
> Catacombs (Lillenas)
> The Case of the Frozen Saints (Baker's Plays)
> The Waiting Room (Baker's Plays)
> A Family Christmas (Contemporary Drama Services)
> The First Church of Pete's Garage (Baker's Plays)
> Home for Christmas (Baker's Plays)

SKETCH COLLECTIONS:
>
> Sixty-Second Skits (with Chuck Bolte; Group Books)
> Void Where Prohibited (Baker's Plays)
> Some Assembly Required (Contemporary Drama Services)
> Quick Skits & Discussion Starters (with Chuck Bolte; Group Books)
> Vantage Points (Lillenas)
> Batteries Not Included (Baker's Plays)
> Souvenirs (Baker's Plays)
> Sketches of Harvest (Baker's Plays)

MUSICALS:
>
> The Meaning of Life & Other Vanities (with Tim Albritton;
>> Baker's Plays)